2
THE MONSTER STORM

story by LOURDES HEUER
pictures by LYNNOR BONTIGAO

Amulet Books • New York

THE SEASHELL KEY SERIES

BOOK 1: Seashell Key
BOOK 2: The Monster Storm
BOOK 3: The Lucky Day

PUBLISHER'S NOTE: This is a work of fiction. Names, characters, places, and incidents are either the product of the author's imagination or used fictitiously, and any resemblance to actual persons, living or dead, business establishments, events, or locales is entirely coincidental.

Cataloging-in-Publication Data has been applied for and may be obtained from the Library of Congress.

ISBN 978-1-4197-6743-2
eISBN 978-1-64700-984-7

Text © 2025 Lourdes Heuer
Illustrations © 2025 Lynnor Bontigao
Book design by Melissa Nelson Greenberg and Becky James

Published in 2025 by Amulet Books, an imprint of ABRAMS. All rights reserved. No portion of this book may be reproduced, stored in a retrieval system, or transmitted in any form or by any means, mechanical, electronic, photocopying, recording, or otherwise, without written permission from the publisher.

Printed and bound in China
10 9 8 7 6 5 4 3 2 1

Amulet Books® is a registered trademark of Harry N. Abrams, Inc.

ABRAMS The Art of Books
195 Broadway, New York, NY 10007
abramsbooks.com

CONTENTS

Act I: The Fall Festival 7

Act II: Guppy School 27

Act III: Scary Stories to Tell in the Dark 43

Act IV: The Monster of Seashell Key 63

ACT 1

THE FALL FESTIVAL

CHAPTER 1

It is the first day of fall on Seashell Key!

On the first day of fall on Seashell Key, the wind blows. Kites sway.

Birds circle and sing.

Clouds gray. Waves crash.

Off the coast, a monster storm is brewing!

But on land, it is calm for now.

All of Seashell Key is out and about.

Neighbors come from all around.

They come from this way and that.

Everyone is here!

Eli, Ezra, and Elana are here.

Sasha and Sophia are here.

Mrs. Cerise is here.

Mateo is here, too!

So is his dad.

Whirr, whirr! Look up!

The Sky and Sea Shop plane flies high above!

Today's banner reads . . .

Some neighbors come to the Fall Festival on Seashell Key for the treats.

There are sea-salted popcorn balls.

There are sea-salted boiled peanuts.

There are sea-salted curly fries.

But Mateo is not here for the treats.

Some neighbors come to the fall festival on Seashell Key for the games.

There is Pick a Rubber Duck.

There is Pin the Backbone on the Sea Slug.

There is Go Fish and Release.

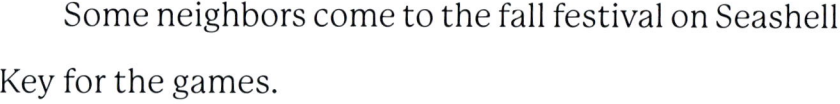

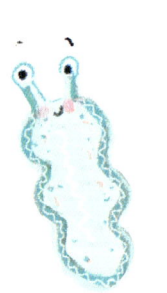

But Mateo is not here for the games.

Some neighbors come to the fall festival on Seashell Key for the contests.

There is a contest for best pie.

There is a contest for best costume.

There is a contest for best scarecrow.

This is why Mateo is here.

Which contest will he enter?

CHAPTER 2

The first contest is for best pie on Seashell Key.

Mateo has never made a pie.

But how hard can it be?

He does not know how to bake.

But he can make a no-bake pie.

He looks at the ingredients.

What kind of pie will Mateo make?

He grabs something sweet.

He grabs something sharp.

He grabs something sour.

He pours and stirs.

He folds and whips.

Ding! Time's up!

Mrs. Cerise judges the competition.

First, she tastes Mateo's pie:

"Banana, cheese, and sour cream. Interesting!"

Then she tastes the second pie:

"Cookies, marshmallow, and mint cream. Delicious!"

She tastes the third pie:

"Vanilla, lime, and coconut cream. Scrumptious!"

"This pie is the winner!"

Mateo can see why.

Who doesn't love lime coconut cream pie?

Still, Mateo thinks: Winning would be nice.

He enters a second contest.

The second contest is for best costume on Seashell Key.

Mateo has never made a costume.

But how hard can it be?

He does not know how to sew.

But he can make a no-sew costume.

He looks at the supplies.

What costume will Mateo make?

He grabs foam balls and googly eyes.

He grabs pipe cleaners and yarn.

He grabs scissors and glue.

He measures and cuts.

He twists and glues.

Ding! Time's up!

Sasha judges the competition.

First, she inspects Mateo's costume.

She says, "Good work, but there's no such thing as monsters."

Sasha is like many grownups. She is a stickler for facts.

Then she inspects the second costume.

She says, "Good work, but there's no such thing as ghosts."

She inspects the third costume.

She says: "Excellent work, and best of all, accurate!"

"This is the winner!"

Mateo can see why.

A dog costume is a very realistic costume.

Still, Mateo wonders: What would it be like to win?

He did not win the pie contest.

He did not win the costume contest.

But there is one contest left!

CHAPTER 3

The third contest is for best scarecrow on Seashell Key.

Mateo has never built a scarecrow.

He looks at the materials.

Surely, he should grab twine and wire. And that he does.

But others also grab sharp garden forks to scare the crows.

Mateo does not grab a garden fork.

They grab loud chimes and bells to jolt the crows.

But Mateo does not grab chimes or bells.

They grab shiny, shiny sea glass to confuse the crows.

But Mateo does not grab shiny, shiny sea glass.

What does Mateo grab instead?

A shirt that looks like a sea of sunflowers.

A box with straw.

One pie pan filled with water.

One pie pan filled with seed.

All around, birds tweet.

They trill.

A blue-gray gnatcatcher swoops in.

Then more.

A white-crowned pigeon lunges.

Then more.

A black-capped chickadee dives.

Then more.

Many birds roost on Mateo's creation.

Ding! Time's up!

Sophia judges the competition.

There are no birds on the first scarecrow.

To be sure, this must be the winner.

But Sophia says, "Not one bird?!"

One bird perches on scarecrow number two.

If the first scarecrow did not win, this one must.

But Sophia says, "Just one bird?!"

And this is how Mateo came to win the third contest on Seashell Key.

For Mateo would never make a scarecrow.

But a no-scare scarecrow: For Mateo, how hard would that be?

And who loves a scarecrow that scares no bird at all?

Sophia, who thought Mateo's scarecrow an avian wonder, a marvel.

It was, she believed, the best, most wonderful, most marvelous kind of scarecrow: the no-scare kind.

ACT II

GUPPY SCHOOL

CHAPTER 1

After the contests, Sasha and Sophia head to the seashore.

They love the seashore even when clouds darken above.

Waves swell.

The storm is closer to Seashell Key.

But it is not here yet.

Lifeguards Leah and Luca make sure everyone is safe.

Lifeguard Leah watches swimmers in the ocean.

Lifeguard Luca teaches swimming lessons in the guppy lagoon.

The guppy lagoon is where Sasha and Sophia learned to swim.

It is where they learned to kick and paddle.

It is where they learned to crawl and float.

But that was a long time ago.

They are not guppies anymore!

Now they are good, strong swimmers.

Still, Sasha loves all kinds of lessons.

She loves science lessons and history lessons.

She loves math lessons and writing lessons.

The only thing she can think of better than learning lessons is teaching them.

Sasha thinks about dog paddling and star floating and makes this suggestion:

"We will teach swim lessons in the guppy lagoon!"

Sophia is not so sure about Sasha's suggestion.

Sophia does not love lessons.

But she does love the water. She does love to swim.

She wonders if teaching lessons to little guppies will be better than learning them.

Lifeguard Luca says, "Let's train you."

He lets them practice teaching in the guppy lagoon.

What lessons do they practice?

CHAPTER 2

"The first lesson of guppy school is . . ." he says.

Sasha interrupts: ". . . Listen to Fish. Don't you remember, Sophia?"

Sophia does not remember.

Grownups teach so many lessons.

Who can remember them all?

Still, Listen to Fish sounds fun.

She wonders which fish will speak to her.

Maybe the snook or the ladyfish.

Sophia puts her ear in the water.

She hears them.

They tell her how the sun feels on their scales, how they dance under the sea.

She takes her ear out of the water.

She tells Sasha what they said.

"No, that's not what Lifeguard Luca means," Sasha says.

"Listen to Fish is about getting used to having water in your ears," she says. "I don't believe fish speak."

But to be sure, Sasha puts her ear in the water.

What does she hear?

It is as she expected.

Sasha hears the gurgle of water, the swishing of fins.

"The second lesson of guppy school is..." Lifeguard Luca says.

Sasha interrupts: "... Talk to Fish. Did you forget, Sophia?"

Sophia did forget.

It is easy to forget so many things, like one's lunchbox or one's homework.

Still, Talk to Fish sounds fun.

Which fish would listen?

Maybe the tarpon or the pompano.

Sophia puts her face underwater.

She talks to the fish.

She tells them to watch out for sea monsters, to be safe in the storm.

She pops her face out of the water.

She tells Sasha what she told the fish.

"No, that's not what Lifeguard Luca means," Sasha says.

"Talk to Fish is about learning to blow bubbles underwater," she says. "I don't believe fish hear."

She puts her own face under the water.

She only blows bubbles.

What would Sasha even tell a fish?

CHAPTER 3

"The third lesson of guppy school is . . ." Lifeguard Luca says.

It is Sophia who interrupts this time.

This time she remembers first. "Catch Fish! That's the best part!"

Sophia is right.

Sasha and Sophia sit side by side on the sandbar.

They reach their arms up in the air.

They plunge them in the water.

They pull in the water, dive in, and . . .

SWIM!

Sasha is a good swimmer, to be sure.

But Sophia is a great one.

She swims out past the sandbar and back in, out past the sandbar and back in.

She never tires.

She swims circles around Sasha.

She puts her arms out and yells:

"Catch Fish!"

She tickles Sasha.

Sasha laughs.

She knows now what she would tell the fish.

Sasha puts her head underwater and says:

"My sister is the best swimmer I know."

Then she gets out of the water.

She grabs her towel. She grabs her pencils. She grabs her journal.

She draws Sophia like a mermaid.

She draws her teaching a school of fish.

She sits and draws until the rain starts and an alarm rings.

The monster storm approaches. Lifeguard Luca says, "Time to get out!"

Sophia says, "Yes, before things get eel-ectric!"

ACT III

SCARY STORIES TO TELL IN THE DARK

CHAPTER 1

That night, the monster storm arrives on Seashell Key.

Eli, Ezra, and Elana take shelter in their lighthouse.

They shut all the windows.

They close the front door.

Their parents keep the light shining out at the sea.

The lighthouse is a beacon in the storm.

Eli, Ezra, and Elana keep themselves busy.

How do they keep busy?

"Let's read secret spy stories," Eli says.

"Let's read space invader stories," Ezra says.

"Let's read bold explorer stories," Elana says.

They have the right idea.

Reading is the perfect way to wait out a storm.

Eli grabs his favorite book.

Ezra grabs his favorite book.

Elana grabs her favorite book.

They sit inside the lighthouse with books in hands when...
CRACK!
BOOM!
POP!

Outside, thunder roars.

Lightning strikes.

The front door blows open.

Pixie hides behind the sofa.

Xena hides under a leaf.

The lights go out!

Eli brings Ezra a blanket.

Ezra grabs Elana's hand.

The lighthouse lamp shines brightly outside across the ocean.

But inside, it is dark.

It is too dark to read stories.

But it is not too dark to tell them.

Eli, Ezra, and Elana know some stories by heart.

Some stories they have heard a thousand times.

One is the story of the monster of Seashell Key.

Eli closes the front door again.

He sits back on the sofa and begins:

"The story of the monster of Seashell Key goes like this..."

CHAPTER 2

This is the story Eli tells:

Once upon a time, secret spies came to the shore of Seashell Key.

They were sent here on a mission.

It was a top-secret mission.

The spies were looking for a monster.

"The monster was a ball of goo!" Ezra says.

"The monster was a kraken!" Elana says.

"No," Eli says.

The monster was a sand serpent.

It was big.

It was scary.

It was sandy.

It slithered under the sand.

Then there was a sandstorm! Sand shifted all around.

But the spies had not brought sand goggles.

They could not see.

So they ran away.

The sand serpent disappeared.

Where did it go?

No one knows.

No one saw the sand serpent ever again.

Does it still lurk somewhere on Seashell Key?

"The end," Eli says.

"No, that's not how the story goes," Ezra says.

"The story of the monster of Seashell Key goes like this..."

Once upon a time, space invaders came to the shore of Seashell Key.

They were sent here on a mission.

It was a top-top-secret mission.

The space invaders were looking for a monster.

"Yes, a sand serpent!" Eli says.

"No, a kraken!" Elana says.

"No," Ezra says.

The monster was a ball of goo.

It was big.

It was scary.

It was green.

It hovered over the sand.

Then there was a goo storm! Goo oozed all around.

But the space invaders had not brought goo goggles.

They could not see.

So they ran away.

The ball of goo disappeared.

Where did it go?

No one knows.

No one ever saw the ball of goo again.

Does it still lurk somewhere on Seashell Key?

"The end," Ezra says.

CHAPTER 3

"No, no, that's not how the story goes either," Elana says.

"The story of the monster of Seashell Key goes like this..."

This is the story Elana tells:

Once upon a time, explorers came to Seashell Key.

They came here on a mission.

It was a top-top-top-secret mission.

The explorers were looking for a monster.

"Right, the sand serpent!" Eli says.

"No, the ball of goo," Ezra says.

"No," Elana says.

The monster was a kraken.

It was big.

It was scary.

It was soggy.

It jumped out of the water.

There was a storm! Water sprayed all around.

But the explorers had not brought water goggles.

They could not see.

So they ran away.

The kraken disappeared.

No one ever saw the kraken again . . .

Where did it go?

No one knows.

"Until now!"

The bathroom door opens.

Elana points!

Pixie jumps in her lap.

Xena sticks her head inside her shell.

Then *CRACK!*
BOOM!
POP!

Lightning flashes.

In the light, they see it is . . . . . . their grandmother!

She stands in the doorway.

She puts on her glasses.

She sends them to bed.

But first she warms glasses of milk.

She makes toast with honey.

She wouldn't send Eli, Ezra, and Elana to bed on empty stomachs.

She's not a monster!

ACT IV

THE MONSTER OF SEASHELL KEY

CHAPTER 1

It is the morning after the first day of fall on Seashell Key.

The storm has passed!

Eli, Ezra, and Elana wake up after a long night of dreaming.

They dreamt of secret spies, of space invaders, of great explorers.

But this is not a dream: The front door is open.

Xena is here.

But where is Pixie?

Pixie is missing!

Eli, Ezra, and Elana do not waste a minute.

They rush out in search of Pixie.

"Maybe she went to Mateo's house," Eli says. "You know she likes to bark at the Sky and Sea Shop plane."

"Maybe she went to Sasha and Sophia's house," Ezra says. "You know she loves their mother's sandwiches."

"Maybe she ran to the beach," Elana says.

"You know her favorite thing is running up and down the seashore."

Eli, Ezra, and Elana set off.

First, they make their way to Mateo's house.

As they approach his house, Eli hears noises. Something caws.

Ezra sees a cloud outside Mateo's house. The cloud is black and white and blue-grey.

Elana points.

What is it?

"The monster of Seashell Key!" they say.

Mateo walks out.

"That's no monster!" Mateo says.

And up close, they see it is not.

It is Mateo's no-scare scarecrow.

Birds perch on floral arms.

They drink and eat from pie-pan feet.

A mama bird nests on a hat of straw.

What a relief.

But Pixie is still missing.

If Pixie is not with Mateo . . .

. . . where could she be?

CHAPTER 2

Eli, Ezra, Elana, and Mateo search for Pixie together.

They are worried.

What if the sand serpent scooped her?

What if the ball of goo oozed her?

What if the kraken took her?

They make their way to Sasha and Sophia's house.

As they approach their house,

Ezra spots a giant fin.

Elana points to something fishy outside Sasha and Sophia's house.

What is it?

"The monster of Seashell Key!" they say.

Sasha walks out.

"That's no monster!"

And up close, they see it is not.

It is Sophia wearing a mermaid costume.

"That is a very realistic costume," Mateo says. What a relief it's not a monster. But Pixie is still missing.

If Pixie is not with Sasha and Sophia, where could she be?

Together, they all go search the seashore.

Lifeguards Leah and Luca are there.

"Sir, ma'am, we are here on a mission," Eli says.

"The mission is to find Pixie," Ezra says.

"The mission is to save Pixie from a monster," Elana says.

Sasha does not believe in monsters.

But there is *something* on the beach.

Could it be the monster of Seashell Key?

CHAPTER 3

It must be.

From far away, they all spot it:

Something sandy.

Something green.

Something soggy.

"See! I was right. The monster of Seashell Key is a slithering sand serpent!" Eli says.

"No! I was right. The monster of Seashell Key is a ball of green goo!" Ezra says.

"No, no! I was right. The monster of Seashell Key is a scary soggy kraken," Elana says.

"Run!" the trio yells.

And they do.

But Sasha yells, "Stop!"

She does not run away.

She is very brave.

She walks up to the monster.

The monster quakes and shakes.

Sand flies everywhere.

Goo flies everywhere.

Water flies everywhere.

Sasha says, "That is no monster! That is . . . PIXIE!"

And up close, they see it is.

Pixie was covered in sand and seaweed and water.

"But how did you know?" Mateo says.

"Like I've said before," Sasha says, "there's no such thing as monsters."

"Now let's go home," she says. "There's homework to finish."

"Homework: Now that's scary!" Sophia says.

Pixie jumps on Eli, Ezra, and Elana. They laugh.

The story of Pixie, the monster of Seashell Key, is a story they will tell again someday.

Some stories you remember by heart.

Mateo and Sophia dip their toes in the water.

They wonder:

"Can we stay and feed the birds?" Mateo asks.

"Yes, can we stay and swim like fish?" Sophia asks.

Could they?

Sasha thinks about it.

She puts her ear to the water.

It gives her the answer:

To be sure, there is homework to finish.

But there is always homework to finish.

The storm has passed.

The mystery of the monster of Seashell Key has been solved.

The sun is shining again.

Yes, they would stay a little longer on the shore of Seashell Key.

ABOUT THE AUTHOR

Lourdes Heuer holds an MFA in writing from the Vermont College of Fine Arts and is an associate professor of English at Broward College in South Florida. She is the author of several books, including *On This Airplane* and *Esme's Birthday Conga Line*. Lourdes grew up in a city apartment above a little toy shop before moving to South Florida, where she spent many of her summers making sandcastles on the shore of the Cape Florida Lighthouse of Key Biscayne.

ABOUT THE ILLUSTRATOR

Lynnor Bontigao is an illustrator based in New Jersey. She is a recipient of the SCBWI Tomie dePaola Award. Lynnor is the author-illustrator of *Sari-Sari Summers* and the illustrator of *You Are Revolutionary* by Cindy Wang Brandt and *The World's Best Class Plant* by Audrey Vernick and Liz Garton Scanlon. Lynnor loves stories where family relationships, culture, and food are intertwined.